Triceratops Stomp

Karen Patkau

pajamapress

First published in Canada and the United States in 2019

Text copyright © 2019 Karen Patkau
Illustration copyright © 2019 Karen Patkau
This edition copyright © 2019 Pajama Press Inc.
This is a first edition.

10 9 8 7 6 5 4 3 2 1

www.pajamapress.ca   info@pajamapress.ca

 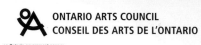

Canada Council Conseil des arts
for the Arts du Canada

ONTARIO ARTS COUNCIL
CONSEIL DES ARTS DE L'ONTARIO
an Ontario government agency
un organisme du gouvernement de l'Ontario

Canadä

The publisher gratefully acknowledges the support of the Canada Council for the Arts and the Ontario Arts Council for its publishing program. We acknowledge the financial support of the Government of Canada through the Canada Book Fund (CBF) for our publishing activities.

Library and Archives Canada Cataloguing in Publication
Patkau, Karen, author, illustrator
Triceratops stomp / Karen Patkau.
ISBN 978-1-77278-079-6 (hardcover)
I. Title.
PS8581.A7839T75 2019   jC813'.54   C2018-905919-2

Publisher Cataloging-in-Publication Data (U.S.)
Names: Patkau, Karen, author.
Title: Triceratops Stomp / Karen Patkau.
Description: Toronto, Ontario Canada : Pajama Press, 2018. | Summary: "A nest of baby dinosaurs hatches deep in the forest and the little dinos immediately begin scampering and playing. When a T-Rex threatens the hatchlings, their fierce mother Triceratops scares it away, and the tired babies settle in for a nap"— Provided by publisher.
Identifiers: ISBN 978-1-77278-079-6 (hardcover)
Subjects: LCSH: Dinosaurs -- Juvenile fiction. | Animal defenses – Juvenile fiction. | Animals -- Infancy – Juvenile fiction. | Stories in rhyme. | BISAC: JUVENILE FICTION / Animals / Dinosaurs & Prehistoric Creatures. | JUVENILE FICTION / Concepts / Sounds. | JUVENILE FICTION / Concepts / Words.
Classification: LCC PZ7.P385Tr | DDC [E] – dc23

Original art created with digital media
Cover and book design—Rebecca Bender

Manufactured by Qualibre Inc./Print Plus
Printed in China

Pajama Press Inc.
181 Carlaw Ave. Suite 251 Toronto, Ontario Canada, M4M 2S1

Distributed in Canada by UTP Distribution
5201 Dufferin Street Toronto, Ontario Canada, M3H 5T8

Distributed in the U.S. by Ingram Publisher Services
1 Ingram Blvd. La Vergne, TN 37086, USA

For Andrew, Adam, and Michael

Nestled in the ferns is a clutch of BIG eggs.

Tap-tap. Peck-peck. Crack. Crack. Crack.

Out pokes a beak! Up pops a head!

Pick-pick! Poke-poke! Pop! Pop! Pop!

Beaks, legs,
tails, and heads

wriggle-wriggle,
squirm-squirm,
S—T—R—E—T—C—H.

Triceratops babies hatch from the eggs.

Chirp-chirp! Cheep-cheep! Peep-peep-peep!

Triceratops babies find something to eat.

Chomp-chomp. Munch-munch. Gulp-gulp-gulp.

From the top of a hill
comes an awful
ROARRR!

Thud-thud. Thud-thud.
Stomp. Stomp. Stomp.

Triceratops babies blink-blink-blink.

uh-oh. Oh-no. EEK! EEK! EEK!

Triceratops mother points her horns.

Stomp-stomp! Sniff-sniff! Snort! Snort! Snort!

Thud-thud. Thud-thud. STOMP. STOMP. STOMP.

T-Rex is here! He's ready to fight!

GROWL-SNARL! HISS-HISS! BELLOWWW!

Mother is FIERCE. T-Rex is afraid.

He turns around and runs away...

THUD-THUD.
Thud-thud.
Stomp. Stomp. Stomp.

Triceratops babies race back home.

Chirp-chirp! Cheep-cheep! Peep-peep-peep!

Nestled in the ferns, Triceratops babies have a rest.

Snuggle-snuggle. Sigh-sigh. Snore. Snore. Snore.

Can You FIND Me in the Story?

I WAS A PLANT-EATING GIANT WITH A VERY LONG NECK AND A TINY HEAD.

AN ARMORED DINOSAUR, I HAD A BIG CLUB AT THE END OF MY TAIL.

ANKYLOSAURUS

ALAMOSAURUS

MY NAME MEANS "HELMETED LIZARD," BUT I WAS A DUCK-BILLED DINOSAUR.

A FLYING REPTILE, I HAD WINGS THAT STRETCHED FROM MY ANKLES TO MY FINGERS.

CORYTHOSAURUS

I RAN FAST AND HAD SHARP TEETH IN MY MOUTH AND DAGGERS ON MY FEET.

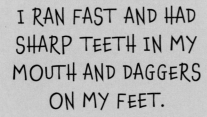

PTEROSAUR

WITH A BODY AS BIG AS AN ELEPHANT, I HAD THREE HORNS ON MY HEAD.

I WAS A FEROCIOUS MEAT-EATER THAT STALKED THE LAND FOR A TASTY MEAL.

DROMAEOSAURUS

TRICERATOPS

TYRANNOSAURUS